MICAH

D. Steven Burns

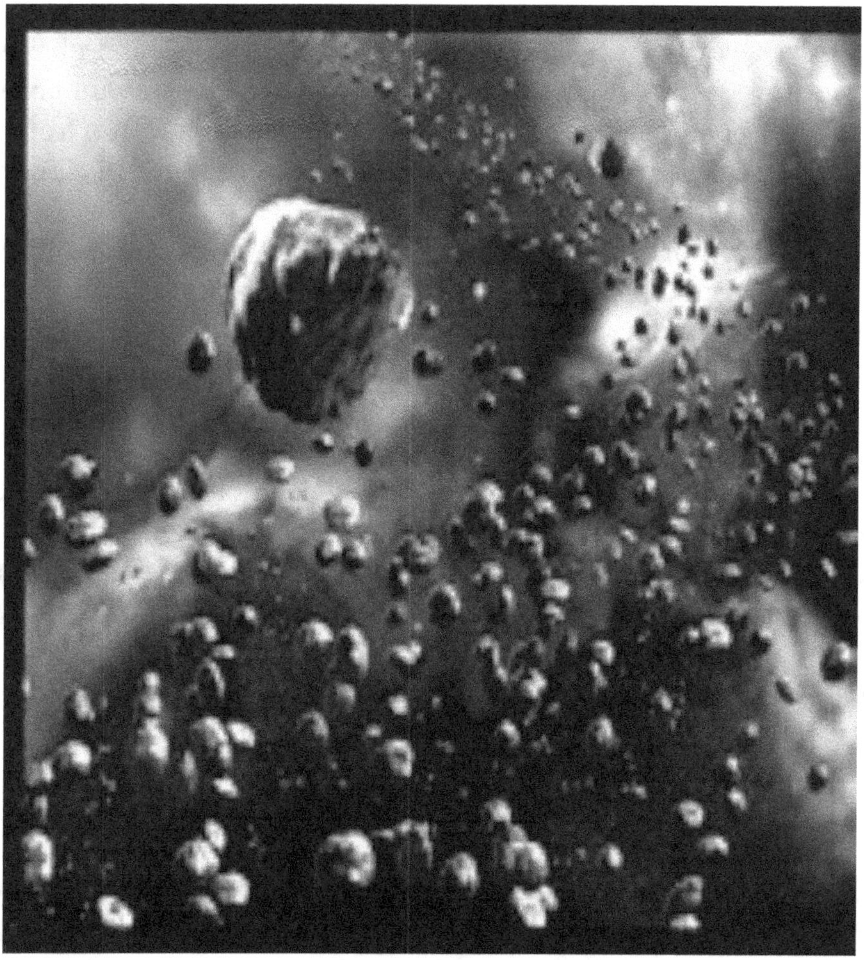

Known space view of the Rift of Joshua

THE RIFT OF JOSHUA

Alero Pruitt's aging mind drifted like the objects visible through the space liner's observation port. Galactic leftovers of varying sizes performed lazy dancing orbits into and around each other; forming and dislodging temporary clusters in slow motion. Periodically one might suddenly out-gas and change direction when the ships lasers were employed to prevent collision. The cosmic choreography was welcome distraction from a week of nearly continuous questions he had thought his fifteen minutes of fame had happened years ago.

"It's almost hypnotic!" Regina Remington's now familiar voice reclaimed his attention. "And quite beautiful until you remember how many lives were lost here," her classic good looks must provide some advantage to her broadcasting carrier. The hovering, darting camera drones had abandoned his notice days ago.

"I'm told it's just a milk run now." The Bishop responded. "Have you been to the rift before?" It was Alero's nature to be engaging with others. His many years in the ministry benefited from his genuine interest in and about others.

The woman smiled. "Actually I covered Quarannum seven years ago. I got to interview several artists including your friend Darrel Hawshaw and Master Escalates before he died. Couldn't get Micah Janice but then no one ever can.

Alero chuckled. "Mica guards his inscrutable genius persona well. Besides he's always crankier during Quarannum"

"My producer told me that, as the first Warp-Artist guild director, you actually started Quarannum."

"Oh yes that. Well we had to get our act together because

the federation was finally noticing our little magic show. Back then anyone with a spaceship and guts could seek out the warp and roll the dice about making it to the other side in one piece. Fools and fortune hunters were perishing in number too big to ignore and the few human minds with the psychic ability and mental discipline required to be safe in the warp were in danger of losing access to it."

"Just a second Bishop Wasn't Quarannum just a massive candidate screening process for warp art apprenticeships. That sort of turned into a festival like, planet-wide celebration? I've been to Quarannum and I can't see how it contributes to warp transit safety?"

The bishop broke into a smile. "Your description has it seemingly promoting more hangovers than safety." They laughed. "The serious selection aspect of Quarannum is only one part of the whole enchilada. That is how we certified artists as fit to face the warp. No certification no warp contact became our, hard and fast, rule. Quarannum was how we developed new talent. Without some opportunity, every four years, the cowboy mentality would still be littering space with bodies. The other part became mental diversion of everyone not making art. It kept the average mind from accidentally engaging the destructive creativity which had killed so many. No matter how many people are in the bath it only takes one to pull the plug. So our transports became so safe that now even the federation enforces a guild monopoly on Warp-transit"

"If that's true, then why are we traveling on a commercial space liner?" she asked.

"It's on your ticket. Alero said pointing to the coded transit tag passengers wore. "We rendezvous with a guild charter for the jump to Loraine" She must have known that.

The interviewer smiled warmly and patted Alero's wrinkled hand. "Sorry bishop I was just trying to prompt you to explain why there is no Transit hub. Most of our viewers will never be here, in the Rift of Joshua, so they can't understand why it remains a risky trip."

"Ahh" Alero nodded "Well if you show some footage of this," the bishop tapped the view port behind him. "It becomes clear pretty fast why. There is no stable body to orbit and no safe piece of space to park a hub station."

Regina laughed and waged a finger at her elderly guest. "Now hang on there." She began. "Don't you think you've had enough jobs without bucking for mine? Although that is a very good idea" she shifted in her lounge seat grabbed the drone controller, and directed one of the tiny flying cameras to capture the outside action. "You have been terrific through these several days. With what we edit of you and some stock footage I think you'll like how it turns out. After your Guild reception we will be out of your hair."

With either a few more years on her or several less on him Alero might have protested the end of her company. He sighed. "Off the record, why is an old clergyman's trip to his retirement home of any genuine public interest?"

Regina tapped purposefully on the controller app of her screen causing the green lights of the camera drones to turn red. "Bishop you are far from a typical retiree. In my trade we say that Public interests focus on the two Fs of Fear and fascination. Warp art generates both with it's terrifying bloody history and Awe inspiring Artists who create from nothing using only their minds. You did that. You organized and protected that. And then you chuck all of it to go seek the will of a more powerful and mysterious creator. Oh and do I need to mention that you were one of the heroes of flight P311a? That is the seminal event that showed the Federation only psychics were safe to handle the warp. An entire transport full of people got to live out their livest only because you and your friends were there."

Regina realized she had a degree of hero worship happening here. She lowered he head and chuckled. "Sorry Bishop I've had my sights on an interview with you for many years. When my producer suggested this special I jumped at the chance." she wasn't ashamed of her own fascination with Warp art and this man in particular. "There may be more colorful people to feature but you are simply and truly one of the most accomplished and honorable men I've ever met."

Alero found her sincerity embarrassing. "It is generous of you to say so. But I'm, just a guy who worked at what was in front of him and wondered about other things. Is there a god? What exactly is a soul? Is it affected by how we act in life? They are quite common speculations, only newsworthy if I figure any of it outo."

"Well bishop I'll want the interview if you do!"

RECEPTION

The planet Loraine deservedly engendered wonder and awe throughout the galaxy.   Not just for being isolated by the rift and warp's, seemingly magical art that made it famous. The place itself seemed contrived perfection. Mostly untouched lush verdant forest carpeted it's surface in hyper vibrant colors. Who knew any natural setting could be so constantly spectacular? But night here was enchanting. The absence of stars made the sky an unimaginable velvet black punctuated only by a single mystical moon traversing the abys like a spotlight on a track.

Regina sighed deeply then turned from that enchanting visage as more people erupted from more air taxis onto the manicured grounds of Stadium Towers. Bishop Pruitt's V.I.P. reception was to be held here; in the single most famous and most massive piece of Warp-art ever produced. As astounding as the achievement was no one had ever claimed credit but then since only one master's abilities so dwarfed contemporaries no one doubted that famous Micah Janis was responsible.

Regina focused on the parade of formally attired guest she was now part of. Approaching the entry, a uniformed guild security officer's presence evoked a memory of this morning's arrival fiasco. Within moments of ground-fall,

Regina had protested when some uniformed fluky grounded her drone cameras; but to no avail. Local news was a function of the Guild archivists who were the only ones authorized to deploy camera-drones at the space-port. As a well known and respected presenter of intergalactic news she had never experienced or expected such interference. "Our law suit will focus on *prior constraint* and this guild will be broke once a Galactic federation Courts rule." she had said with exaggerated indignity.

"I'm really sorry miss Remington but we're not a Federation planet." Federation law held no sway here. " Personally I love your work and am honored to meet you but these drones don't have our local frequencies so property and personal damage is a real probability if we let them fly. You just need Guild approvals and we can provide frequencies later" the young woman was so genuine that The veteran reporter felt foolish for the confrontation.

"Oh! Ah please forgive my tone. That actually makes sense" she said "ok then How quickly can I get those approvals because the subject of my feature is about to exit this ship any second now"

"You'll miss the welcome then because there is no way." the uniformed women held up a hand to Regina's anticipated protest. "We can get you access to our drone footage for this welcome but you'll have to talk to security about any other public drone use. Now let me get you with the welcoming committee so you at least don't miss it"

There had been no point in further dispute. planet Loraine's principal reality seemed to be that the WARP ARTISTS' GUILD runs absolutely everything! However This young employee seemed to be genuinely trying to mitigate the bureaucratic disaster. Regina acquiesced, "Lead on then" she remembered saying.

This evening Regina enjoyed cooperation from the highest level of guild security. Neither her or the GBC drones were challenged upon entering. Inside a cadre of similarly uniformed people awaited guests. One uniformed woman stepped toward Regina but was hailed by an other before she corralled the reporter. "I'll take this one Millie; we have a history." the familiar guard said.

Without breaking stride the girl captured Regina's elbow and headed toward one side of the function hall. ”Bishop Pruitt is in suit C with some of his former colleagues and director Daniels Using the frequencies we provided you we've directed two of the three drones you sent for background into that more private reception so you won't have missed anything. You can, of course, redirect them as you choose. Security chief Hutchinson also assigned me to assist you with anything. He particularly suggested that you might like me to identify guests; you being a stranger here and all”

“I could use that but won't I look silly with you hanging over my shoulder whispering in my ear all evening?”

“Probably!” the guard said presenting a mini ear piece as they walked.

“Oh! that will work.” Regina inserted the device into her left ear. “I must say your guild is being most accommodating”

“Even the guild benefits from good publicity” The younger woman smiled and guided them beyond another guarded door into business suite where people were milling around in conversational knots. “These people are either Guild big-wigs or Master Warp-Artists. All surviving Guild founders are all in this room. Tonight is the first time in a quarter century that can be said.”

“Micah Janis is Here?” Reflexively Regina's head jerked up and around to seek the legendary psychic. What a coupe it would be to get him digitized.

“Yes. I'm told he's here somewhere and Master Hawshaw too. Now I'll trail you at a distance and mention the names and functions of people you encounter ”

Deep breath Regina told herself. Usually she would have been on a first name basis with several significant people at any function. Not here. Loraine was separated from the entire human diaspora by more than just the Warp's mysteries or the Rift's murderous past. These were renown psychic magicians practicing a lethal almost miraculous art; not your garden verity socialites. Glancing around she spotted the bar. Well now she knew her first stop.

Collecting her drink Regina noticed a young man intensely engaged with his personal screen. Was a room full of famous people not an occasion deserving of more personal presence? She wondered. She suddenly recognized the application on that screen and became instantly suspicious. "Excuse me" she said. "You aren't controlling my drones are you?"

Before the young man could answer a familiar voice in her ear said " Randell Parington Guild archivist and a super tech nerd"

"your drones?" he glanced up casually but sprang to attention flustered "Oh Miss Remington. No mam. Guild drones only." he paused drawing in a deep centering breath then swallowing the excess fluid suddenly in his mouth. "Apologies, I'm a huge fan and sort of star struck right now."

Regina laughed. It hadn't occurred to her that among these remarkable people she might be a celebrity. "In this company I'm the grouppy not the band" she said looking around.

"With fame influence and good looks, how often aren't you the center of attention? You honestly have mine." he flushed slightly and paused lifting the screen toward her. "No see I have seven drones working tonight. that's the most I ever use other than Quarannum. And while yours show up too they are yellow on my display. I can monitor but not control them"

"Oh yes I see. Then that's a ten drone control app I've never done more than four." there was admiration in her voice.

"Well your the star as well as the journalese. I'm heavy into the tech end and honestly the Ap's A.I. Handles it as well as I ever could."

"I suspect you are being a bit modest Mr Parington" said Regina extending her hand.

"oh please just Randal or Rad is my nickname but how?"

Regina turned her head and touched the nearly invisible ear piece. "I'm cheating" she smiled.

"I see. To me that's not cheating; just practical forethought."he again glanced at his control app. One of your drones seems to be abandoning Master Pruitt and spending time with other notables."

"background is important in commercial documentaries." said Regina pulling out her own screen "Oh it's sighted a founder"

Rad also studied the Regina's screen, "Ah yes, Master Hawshaw."

Regina had been a journalist too long not to notice self-editing. He had stopped himself from saying something. "What's the matter with him being here?" she asked

Randal clearly wavered over weather or not to answer. "well" he began, "it's just a rumor. It might be untrue as many gossips are and there is no way to confirm it, well maybe one but I would hate for you to do that."

"Rad I'm lost in the jungle of your words here. What are you talking about?"

"You can't broadcast it"

"Can't or Shouldn't?"

"ok out of decency shouldn't."

"Well I'm a fairly decent person and enjoy a professional reputation for discretion. Does that work for you?"

After additional internal struggle Rad spoke quietly. "They say he has less than a month left as an artist"

"Is he dying?" Regina studied the man in the drone's field of vision. "He's walking with strength and other than the normal age lines in the face He looks good."

"his physical health isn't the problem. They say he is loosing Postulation integrity"

Regina struggled to make sense of Randell's statement. Literally Postulation meant thinking or speculating. But in Warp Art it was formalized into a documented process. If art plans filed were **Postulation Sequences** and isolation chambers on the creative flights were **Postulation chambers** than **postulation integrity** must mean the degree to which the final art matched the filed sequential plan. "His art is getting sloppy?" she asked steeling an other look at the screen.

"that's the rumor but even if it's true it's all hush hush."

"I seem to recall hearing the Guild is quick to ground artists who's work isn't exactly what they planned down to the last detail." the reporter offered.

"absolutely" Randell said with assurance. "that is why I personally disbelieve it and hesitated to even mention it. The other thing is that there is no official guild protocol for just saying **O.K. dude your done in a month. Make it count"**

They were laughing at Rad's parody of guild authority when a new voice broke in. "Miss Remington yet again I think I want what the two of your are drinking. Regina recognized the guild security Chief who nodded toward Randell. "no drone crashes so far I hope?"

"no sir we have them frequency balanced" Randal held up his screen for perusal.

Regina extended her hand to the newcomer. "Blyth is it?" her earpiece had already informed her.

"Good memory" he said I thought you'd be trailing the bishop"

"This shindig is in his honor. Besides I've got time slated before my flight tomorrow although I'm getting good footage from my drones. And yours too for which I thank you. Randal and I were just assuring each other of our drones well being. You have an asset in his technical know-how."

"the guild is lucky that way, we get to pick from the best professionals. Most never leave Loraine but those that do do well. It turns out that Guild employment is a sought after credential."

"I am hoping to get your boss digitized later regarding the homecoming of the first man to hold his job.

Blyth sipped the drink he had just accepted. Regina notice that Randell had returned his attention to the drone controls. "ahh Director Daniels frequently mentions Director Pruitt's deft and decisive interventions which kept the Art and Loraine from Federation control. I'm sure he'll make some time later for you in fact I'll mention it to him later."

The man's eyes were darting around the room he was clearly already somewhere else in his head. "Thanks again for all your help" Regina said.

"ahh certainly we are pleased to have you" he spoke without looking at her before he sauntered off.

Regina interrupted her new acquaintance. "Rad what are my chances with Director Daniels?"

"Oh excellent!." he said. "Your the main stream media which formulates public opinion about warp art. He'll consent." the archivist paused. He'd prefer to be interviewed as a Master artist not guild administrator."

Regina was confused. "he's an artist too?"

"No he's not; but he should be"

"weren't most Lorainians Warp art candidates once I can't interview them all." said Regina

"it's True enough that most people had to settle for less than they came here to achieve. but Jack Daniels was famous before he ever got to Loraine. On his home world he was a psychic prodigy. He is the only man to eclipse the record master Micah made in his training. So everyone knew he was coming to Loraine and were positive he'd be just as great"

"Really? so why is he pushing papers today"

because he only pledged to Master Janis who refuses to take apprentices. He did that three times. Scuttlebutt is that Micah promised him who ever he pledged to would take him on. May be he did or may be not but Daniels wouldn't pledge to anyone else so here we are. The guild has never run so smoothly but what has the art lost as a result?"

"Wow! You seem to be a fan of your director."

"can't hide that" he said. "More a fan of people reaching their potential. I'ld hate to have been kept a scree repairman rather than an archivist."

Rad had a good point about potential. What if she had been held to local fill in reporter? Her screen alarm sounded she had set it to announce warp Master Micha Janice and it was. A knot of four people was shown heading toward a corner lounge the bishop with his great niece who Regina had met at the space port, and Masters Hawshaw and Janice. This required her attention.

"Randal I've truly enjoyed our conversation. She again offered her hand. "I'll seek out your footage later but right now I'm on the job." Regina gulped a last sip and abandoned he drink and her new acquaintance.

PICKING UP THE PIECES

An observer might suspect a hypnotist was in front of Aaron Milford moving something shiny in a circle. He checked the com-link board, hold status panels, double S grid cameras, and view port, in one continues loop. Other cargo masters dispensed with the double S on the Lorainian side of the Warp since the hold pods were firefly bright against the black velvet absence of stars. His colleagues called him, "a bit anal." He didn't care. Frankly he wasn't comfortable without exact special positioning information when or if a problem cropped up.

It was the return leg of the Guild charter fifty one and everything seemed five by five. The collection pods were performing their normal post-warp duties in the graceful ballet perfected by decades of protocol and practice.

1)   Collection Pods (adapted shuttle craft) emerge from the cargo holds, winking colored heading lights.
2)   They collect the art objects floating near the ship in their assigned grid spaces.
3)   Then return to the holds with clamps and nets full of the mind-magic collaborations between this galactic anomaly and the artists skilled enough to use it.
4)   Afterwards the Warp-Art would be matched to the postulation papers filed by the transit-chambered artists.

This stable Einstein-Rose-bridge seemingly existed only to support Warp-Art. As theorized, the Warp was a direct connection to and from the part of the universe Humans had colonized. Original explorers had succumbed to the dangers of thinking at the point of warp. Obviously now, we knew better than to allow that. Before the psychics came warp transit had been a one hundred percent fatal undertaking. They developed a simple method of over stimulating the non-engaging areas of the brain. Safe warp transit was born.

Aaron's musings were cut short. "Damn NO!' spat out of the speaker in front of the him. His eyes jerked to the com-link panel and then the Double S grid. It was pod 12

"Finius is that you?" he asked

"Ahhh yah! Get a medical team to my hold on the double I coming in hot"

The hold panels showed twelve still red. "Negative twelve that hatch hasn't been cycled for entry yet"

"Well find me one that is cause we got a problem big time"

Checking the board he found a green light on 17, "you are go for seventeen; that is one seven and there is a pod still parked forward there too. Do you copy?"

"Got it," barked the speaker ", you better tell the guild rep and XO galiger to get there too."

"Ok Finius you know it's your butt if this isn't critical."

"Don't worry; just get emergency medical first"

Aaron made the COM connections. He had spaced with Finius for many years and trusted both his judgment and his piloting skills. Hopefully Finius's emergency still left him with a clear head and steady hands. An impaired operator would have problems with an occupied hold

By the time the pod maneuvered into hold seventeen an anxious medical team huddled under the aft inspection catwalk.

They waited for the outer airlock hatch's pressure to equalize. The precaution was needed because the collection pod assigned to hold seventeen's was resting in place so that maneuvering in an extra pod would be tricky at best. The inner doors opened and the pod was coming in net first and high. The grappling arm was dead center, above the net, holding artwork appearing uniformly white and vaguely sausage shaped. Medical emergency or not the operator was deftly guiding his craft clear of P17 toward an open space closer in.   Once inner hatch magnetic seals engaged gravity plates became active. The team jogged toward the cockpit to confront the emergency.

Motion at P12's grappling arm caught Dr. Heraldson's eye. The captured art had crumpled over on itself. The ship's gravity must have affected it.   Who made flexible art? Ahead the pod pilot was quickly scrambling down the cockpit ladder pausing to gesture urgently toward the grappling arm. He was not appearing unhealthy in the slightest. A second exam of the art brought a horrifying realization.

"That's not product." The doctor said. "That's an occupied Maintenance suit," He deftly altered the group's direction in mid stride toward the grapeler. The suit was indeed occupied. The doctor could see a young man through the face-plate. The pod operator hurried aft to the cargo arm controls and waited for the med team.

When they took hold of the encased body Finius released the pincer fingers. There was nothing more for him to do. He watched the activity of cutting suit, applying detectors and simulators, announcing readings following instructions. All movements seemed calm and purposeful but adrenaline was heightened in all of them. He could see the skipper entering and approaching the team. He must have preempted the executive officer and come himself. The doctor was recycling cortical and cardiac stimms for the third time and cursing.

Thinking better of interrupting the doc Captain Haskell moved to his pod pilot. "Outside during Warp??" he asked eliciting a shrug from Finius.

"Can't say He was in grid 241 by 90 but I was pretty shook up when I realized what it was. I might be off a couple of degrees either way."

The captain Grunted acknowledgment and returned his attention to the med team. The suit was mostly cut away now and stims were clear on the young man's naked chest and head. Captain Haskell was one who took pride in knowing his entire crew; but this face was unfamiliar to him. He tapped the com-link on his collar.

"Yes Captain?"

"Tell our Guild flight rep, I think its Samuelson this time, to get a wiggle on. He's got a pod load of cyber work in hold seventeen. He might need security too but that's his call."

"Yes Sir right away"

"This is not doable "said the doctor. His medics paused in their work awaiting orders. "I'm calling it" he glanced at his chronometer "fifteen forty-four Presented Deceased Unresponsive" The medics rocked backwards onto their heels from their tasks. Each rose showing a variety of emotions on their faces. "Get him chilled and use precautions I need dermal and mucusmembrane full spectrum testing.

"My people will want what's left of the suit to test," said the captain

"Sure if and when I can rule out a pathogenic cause Of Death."

"Good enough. We can wait."

"Wait for what," asked the arriving Guild Rep

"Nice of you to, join us Samuelson. The dock just called a P.D.U. on this kid in the extra vehicular maintenance suit who, just for the record, isn't one of mine. The dock wants the body and I want the suit so we can each know what happened. He won't release the suit until he's sure there's no danger of contagion." The captain looked to the Doctor. "Did I miss anything?"

"Nailed it!" said the dock but his attention quickly shifted to his team preparing to move the body. "Not like that everything needs to be bagged, basted, and blown first including the Hold, the Pod, and all of us.'

"Hold on doctor I just walked in the door" protested Samuelson

The doctor shrugged without much sympathy as he taped his own com-link. "Hold 17 level three precautions seven animates, one P D U, and environmental" turning to the captain he asked, "How could he not be one of yours?"

"Level three?" questioned a disembodied voice

"Absolutely" responded the doctor

"Yah" echoed Samuelson, "What's a P.D.U. And how could he not be one of your crew?"

One of the medics spoke over his shoulder. "Presented dead and unresponsive"

"How indeed? That's why you might want security notified," said the captain. "He's not mine so who is he and how did he get here on a Guild chartered Warp transit? How big are the security holes he snuck through and how much danger are we all in because they exist? Hell we don't even know if he was diverted or tried facing the warp open minded"

"Ok O.K. "Samuelson interrupted horrified at the thought of a naked mind facing the warp. "I get it. I do." After again surveying the seen he continued, "Well someone in the stadium towers will be sorting this one out. I'll feed them details as we get them but I don't envy whoever has this land in their lap."

DUBBLE DEAD DARREL

Security director Blithe Hutchinson brushed wrinkles from his lap while awaiting his boss's response. Jack Daniels stared blankly disbelieving what he had just heard. No punch line followed, no mitigating explanation so apparently Blithe intended for him to believe the preposterous, impossible and just plain dumb statement offered. Neither man moved for several seconds until the director shook his head, raised his palm momentarily and then flexed two of his fingers in a beckoning motion. "I don't believe I heard that " he said

"You know we didn't report the EVA suited fatality from Warp transit fifty four, only the founding master's death." Repeated Blithe

"I got that Darrel Hawshaw somehow died in postulation. We are waiting on the autopsy to close that one. He was ninety-one and working off his thirty day grounding papers any way. It's a big loss but not big trouble." The guild director paused, "I thought I just heard you say that the John Doe body in the EVM suite was Darrel"

"Yes sir I did"-said Blithe

"Well????"

"That one was Darrel Hawshaw too"

"Ehrr…" The director groaned. He didn't like being confused and until just now, had the utmost confidence in his security chief. "I don't think I'm being unreasonable in asking WHICH ONE OF US IS NUTS?" Jack's voice rose in volume and pitch. "Because either I'm hallucinating or you're crazy."

"Sir the retinal and fingerprint patters are exact matches to what we have on file plus there are these " Blythe slid hard copy images of the autopsy photos and a two-D, news archive, stills of a younger Master Darrel Hawshaw across the desk.

After ping-pong examination of the photos and reports, unreasonable and nuts left the room only impossible remained as fact.   It was obviously and scientifically the same man. Jack pressed the com-link on his desk "I need an encrypted quantum conference call with the three best theoretical physicists you can find me; and I need that yesterday. Oh and get me Harper at the spaceport," he ordered.

"Yes sir" replied the desk.

Jack Denials sat back in his chair, covering his face with overly large hands he seemingly tried to wipe away the converging feelings of urgency, confusion, and fear welling up inside him. "You know Blithe I wouldn't like this as a riddle but having to deal with it as a fact just scares the hell out of me."

"Shouldn't it?" asked Blithe, "I can't guess at any cause that doesn't mess with my ideas of what the Warp, or   for that matter, the whole dammed Universe, actually allows. I was sort of hoping you'd find some way to convince me that I was wrong or even flat out nuts"

"We should be so lucky," said Jack "And you're right if our sanity isn't suspect than a universe where this can happen might just be whacko," the director tried to mentally regroup. " So who else knows"

"We may have lucked out there," Blithe began," the tech that brought me the Doe sample chuckled at how stupid Medical had been to mislabel the specimens. Of course then I thought he was right but it just didn't digest well. So I went there for a second set of Doe samples and personally transported them to a different tech for spectrum only. I ran the search, which pulled up Darrel as a match, and it was me on the rentals as well.   Best guess is we may have two days before Process Review can find the data and they"

Blythe was interrupted by the desk com-link. "I have director Harper on line six for you and I'm shooting for your QE_ conference call at 11:00 our time"

"Thank you Anne" Jack raised an index finger to his chief of security and depressed line six. A sun baked face with ample laugh lines appeared on the screen. "Frank how are you"

"Fine Sir," responded the image.

"By now I'm sure you've heard about Master Hawshaw's passing"

"Well yes" Frank hesitated. "There is scuttlebutt that there's something fishy about it but my people tell me your reps won't let them talk I was just about to call you to gripe about that when Anne rang me"

"Oh Frank I apologize for that I absolutely would not exclude you on purpose. It all happened so fast I just plain forgot to tell you. The truth is that, Darrel being a Founder, we wanted to manage the news of his passing and memorials to control any panic."

"Panic?" inquired the phone

"Sadly yes," confirmed Jack. He was now relaxing into the fabrication as the legitimate points he could hang it on became clearer to him. "You don't have to deal with the Federations paranoia about Warp art on a daily basis as I do but I'm sure you're aware of it. I know you understand the deep terror people have for an UN-diverted or impaired mind facing the warp"

"Well yes but"

Jack interrupted, "Frank if Darrel had died in bed I wouldn't have needed to control fear but he didn't. He died in a Postulation chamber on one of our charters. He died an old man of diminishing mental powers facing the most destructive and creative force in the universe and what you didn't know is that I should have grounded him outright but out of respect we gave him 30 day papers."

"OH! " a pause "Shit" an other pause "I see there is a lot of managing to do " said Frank.

Jack could see Blythe nodding approval of the tactic. "This isn't just to cover the Guild's ass Frank although that is an outcome I'm not unhappy with. We can't feed the Federation politicos any excuse to take us over or panic the public"

"Damn!" was the only response

"O K so that brings you into the loop" said Jack. "As director I'm declaring a three day morning period for Master Hawshaw during which I'm making your job easier. No flights out for three days and landing rights are denied for anything not already in transit for the same period. It is an honor demanded by the death of one of the last living founders and we needn't tarnish his reputation with the rest of it"

"I see that," said Frank, "My job may be easier tomorrow but today there are a lot of Q.E calls to be made. Shutting down a space-port isn't a matter of just throwing a switch"

"I'm sure of that and grateful to have you on the job. Remember this is all just to honor a fallen founding master should any press ask"

"I've got it Boss," said Frank, "and thanks for bringing me up to speed."

"Sorry I ever forgot to keep you informed Frank. You take it easy now"

"Sure thing"

Jack returned his attention to Blythe. "Process review" he prompted.

"I was saying it will take them a couple of days to find the unassigned tests and they might even assume they were control runs"

Then it's probably nice they are non-essentials on the administrative leave I'm declaring for the official morning period isn't it?

Blythe smiled at Jacks remarkable mind. "You saw all that before you called Frank didn't you "

Jack shrugged.

"It was brilliant playing the Federation take-over card. Hell they've always been freaked out because physicists can't explain the Warp itself let alone Warp Art. To the public we pull trinkets out of nowhere. The federation worries that we are fiddling with dimensional integrity and has always wanted control," said Blithe.

"All true," said Jack, the early Artists learned all the wonderful and deadly secrets of the Warp long before the federation took notice. By the time they did try to take over we had the first wave of greats like our late master Hawshaw, Escalates, Janice and our recently returned Bishop Pruitt who actually organized the Guild."

"I didn't know that Pruitt was ever an artist let alone a Guild founder," commented Blithe. And how could Micah Janice be a founder when he pays no attention to our protocols?"

"OH yes the bishop might have rivaled our best had he kept at it., The guild was actually young master Micah Janis's idea, your observation notwithstanding. He pushed the others into founding a guild. He also convinced Alero Pruitt to take the helm as first director."

"Nothing personal boss but most of us would give up body parts to be a top Warp artist. Why in hell would Pruitt chuck the money and fame for your job?"

"Ever hear of the P311.a transit?" asked Jack

"Who hasn't? A lunatic terrorist prevented diversion at warp. All the psychics helped but Micah Janis handled the crazy and got most of the public credit! Is that why all you directors let him flaunt the rules that you just insisted he established?"

"Check that resentment Blythe! You know I own more real estate there than anyone" Jack didn't elaborate. "Yes Micah was the organizer but his two lieutenants were Hawshaw and our recently returned Bishop. The terrorist's death never sat right with Pruitt. Clearly he's always been a spiritual man. Anyone that sincerely seeks god isn't too impressed with fame. I bet he thinks he went to a better job in the clergy."

"When you put it that way it does make sense." Blithe said

"The Federation's itchy fingers are our biggest threat here." Jack brought them back on point. "What will they make of two Darrel Hawshaw's both dead and separated in age by fifty or sixty years? They will want to know, and we need to figure out, if it's a time phenomena we hadn't anticipated. Will it, or even can it, ever happen again? Was it inter-dimensional? Could we be poking holes in the very fabric of space-time? Did Darrel the old build Darrel the young in some perverse hope of immortality? Unknowns feed paranoia to federation bureaucrats"

"I know chief" Blithe responded, "If we can't keep the Double Dead Darrel thing quiet, we are on quicksand with this."

"Cute Blythe," Jack said. Did that just pop out or have you been hoping to use it in a sentence all day?"

Blithe smiled despite the gravity of their situation. "I couldn't help it boss." He became serious again. "You mentioned Master Janis. He holds chamber reservations for both directions on tomorrow's flight. Won't he gripe?"

"I don't think so," said the director thoughtfully. "As cantankerous as he is Darrel was his only real friend on Lorain; Well until Bishop Pruitt showed back up. He'll honor the mourning period but we have to try keeping the rest of this under wraps, if that's possible. Hell it may be out there already. This planet has lots of psychics"

Blithe chuckled. "Let's hope we're still prescient enough to out maneuver the Federation again."

"To quote the Bishop, AMEN to that brother" said Jack.

GRAVE SUSPISIONS

"Amen" repeated the mourners when the Bishop finished the service. After a moment they turned by ones and threes to each other in subdued voices. Most thanked Bishop Pruitt for a lovely service. Some braved the scowling visage of Master Micah Jannis who remained immobile in a seat near the grave. Their condolences generated only terse replies from his grief. On this occasion, the Press had the good manners to remain inconspicuous.

People seem to abandon interment sights reluctantly, unsure if sufficient challenge to death had been offered or value to the lost life established. At length all had trickled away accept Micah, Alero Pruitt and his great niece Laura who knew better than to offer platitudes to the older men. She waited patiently as did Alero. Not for the first time, she noted how everyone, choosing the company of Micah, awaited his lead in most things. It would have been her choice to stand nearer to him than her uncle but satellite and news camera drones would surely be trained on them. She could wait.

Micah slapped both palm onto both knees and rose suddenly. "It smells!" he spat

"Micah he was old. We may not be far behind him," protested his friend the bishop.

"He wasn't drop dead old," Micah was indignant. "Come on Alero I know we psychics avoid poking into each other's minds but we can't help sensing the basics. He was healthier than me." Micah gestured toward Laura "just ask the Empath here," both men awaited her input

"Last Tuesday, Master Hawshaw had no serious pathology. He was particularly healthy and I should add excited by more than just your home-coming reception," she confirmed.

"Told yah!" Micah said walking from the gaping dirt maw soon to swallow his friend. "I wouldn't expect Laura to know but you've faced the Warp; do you think anything could stop a postulation sequence once triggered?

The Bishop became speculative before answering. "Probably not" he admitted

"So ware is Darrel's art piece? I tell yah it stinks and double stinks!"

"I can't figure it Micah," his friend said after a moment. "In my work, I guess, I sort of accept a purpose to things without too much questioning."

"Well question this" Micah interrupted, "Why is Darrel's apartment under quarantine?"

"I heard nothing about that". Alero said scratching his head. "It doesn't seem to jive with the assessments you and Laura just gave. Do you suppose they think he died of something contagious?"

"If they believed that the G-MED teams would have been in there already." Micah paused. "No Daniels and his laky Blithe Hutchinson are hiding something pretty big. Besides Darrel wasn't the only death on that flight". Micah remembered overhearing a pod operator from fifty-one, Finius something was his name, talking about a body he'd mistaken for art. Intoxicated and clearly upset, the man was explaining that *no one even knew the poor kid's name*. Instantly a lump had formed in Micah's stomach, his pulse pounded in his ears and his face flushed crimson. The two Warp-transit deaths were somehow related. Objective support for that conclusion was absent but intuition had always served him well. Micah was positive he needed to know more about the other death before any sense could be made of Darrel's. Micah explained, "An art pod scooped some young maintenance worker up, from that same flight, but do we here anything about that from anywhere? Not a peep!"

How would you know that if they are keeping it quiet?" Alero asked.

"Because a Warp death scares the crap out of spacers and they drink and bitch on a fairly regular basis"

Sensing the rising anxiety, Laura stepped between the two men insinuating her arms around their elbows. "I'm sure you'll each find answers but I don't see them lying around here" she said

Micah frowned at her arm in his but noted it could look like the younger generation simply being solicitous of Elders. He mentally shrugged. She always felt damn good next to him.

The three entered the waiting air-cab. It would take them to the reception at Laura's home. "1327 Sagamore Terrace" she said. As the ground retreated from them Bishop Alero Pruitt was questioning the wisdom of returning to this planet and this life after so many years. Laura Pruitt reflected on how foolish, challenging, strange, sad, and wonderful emotions were. She wondered when, or how, she'd tell her uncle. Warp Master Micah Janice sought to name the nagging discomfort in his gut, which was more than loss, sadness, or shock. The discomfort in his ears was more easily named. Air's pressure diminished with altitude causing inner ears to expand painfully.

"ASSENDING TO CLEAR MOUNTIANS, AUDITORY DISCOMFORT IS POSSIBLE. WOULD YOU CARE FOR SOME GUM??" asked the computerized taxi speaker. A small steel drawer popped open on the forward panel. The bishop took a piece. Laura and Micah declined simply forcing exaggerated yawns to cope. There seemed nothing useful to say. They each settled deeper into separate seats, separate thoughts, and separate silences.

GUMMED UP ALIBY

"But master Janis I did give you the postmortem DNA reports of that young John Doe." The guild lab clerk insisted.

"I have 2 reports of the same sample!" accused Micah, who expected more competence for his bribe. "I'm holding them both in my hand and they are exactly the same. See," Micah shoved the hard copies toward the phone.

"Ah OH Yes!" stuttered the man. "They do seem the same."

"SEEM THE SAME," yelled Micah. "The only differences are the labels John Doe, and Darrel Hawshaw"

"I can only tell you it wasn't my error," explained the image ", that is what I got from the files. Now if they gave me master Hawsjaw's records twice by mistake that's not my fault," He pleaded. "Also you calling me here is just begging for trouble. Let me see what I can find out and I'll contact you later" he offered.

Micah broke the connection with a snarl. The gnawing unease still bothered him. Was he supposed to believe both bodies were Darrel? Sudden comprehension scalded him like boiling water. He could feel a terror gaining strength within him. What if there was no mistake? Each sample was truly Darrel one sixty years younger than the other. Micah should have recognized the John Doe photos as his college friend instantly. "Oh my God" Micah vocalized. Hutchinson and Denials must already know. That explains the news black out on the matter. Suddenly the lab clerk's fears of being caught switched from paranoid to probable. Micah would have to cover his tail and establish a plausible alibi;

and fast!

He had been foolish to call from his own condo's phone. How could he get out of this? In his head, Micah paused momentarily and awaited the plan he knew would emmerge. Unbidden, intricate and comprehensive, it emerged. One moment horrified shock and the next in motion executing the sequence now complete in his mind. Quickly he reviewed what was needed. The drug wasn't illegal as such but use of it by Warp artists was supposed to be documented and restricted to several days prior to any postulation chamber booking. The tool and data chip were unremarkable and since the woman was inexplicable dedicated to him, it should all work out.

Micah spun the phone so even guild security video override would only catch the wood grain paneling. He injected the drug into a conveniently prominent vein on his upper thigh and took several deep breaths to mitigate the rush, which could leave many his age, unconscious. The unnatural strength conferred came from adrenaline and stored sugars pouring into the blood stream. Sliding the chip and tool into his front and back pocket respectively, he walked out to the balcony studied the handholds he'd need and began his ascent as the phone's insistent chirping began. The lab tech had ratted him out already.

Micah was three balconies over and thirteen up shaking violently. What else could he expect being this out of shape, this old, and this juiced up. The air taxi approached Sam Blumenthal's balcony precisely on time. Sam was a man of exact habits. Fortunately one was always being exactly four minutes behind schedule. Micah dove into the cab before Sam could know it was even there. In a clear voice he said ", 1327 Sagamore Terrace" the taxi lifted off for the 20 minute flight. Micah began dismantling the autopilot containment barrier on the front panel. He used the maintenance inputs to download the pickup and delivery log data to his chip. He then replaced the Blumenthal call with one for Janis and swapped the pickup time with a fair two hours prior.

Last he uploaded the doctored log back to the taxi computer and reinstalled the panel confident that this part of his alibi was established.

Only after leaning back did he realize that his ears hurt. More than that the adrenaline was dissipating, the shaking was still bad, plus he was strangely, and uniformly warm all over. On top of this feeling of being slowly micro waved, a bone aching tired was enveloping him. Micah slumped warily back into the seat with a heavy sigh.

"ASSENDING TO CLEAR MOUNTIANS, AUDITORY DISCOMFORT IS POSSIBLE. WOULD YOU CARE FOR SOME GUM??" the taxi popped open It's steel gum drawer.

Too fatigued to muster a good yawn, Micah reached for gum. His weary arm seemed three times its normal weight and the trembling finger found only an empty drawer. Exasperated he yelled, "NO GUM". Instantly the drawer slammed closed; it's steel biting into his trapped digit. The pain shot him out of his slumped position toward fully erect, which the vehicle had no room to accommodate. The head blow on the roof produced brightness before dizzying blackness and temporary loss of body control. He fell toward the left twisting his wrist and finger even more painfully. Unbidden a screech emerged from his throat.

"Are you injured or ill?" Asked the taxi's speaker

"Let go of my finger!" Micah bellowed unable to free himself from the trap.

"Abnormal speech patterns detected are you injured or Ill?" It repeated

"Of course I'm injured you mechanical sadist let me go?" Micah was suddenly propelled into the front panel as all forward momentum ceased. The machine swung itself around one hundred eighty degrees violently swinging Micah leftward against the door. He felt the finger snap shooting pain up to his elbow.

The taxi accelerated back toward the spaceport at high speed jerking him into a twisted knot of arms and legs.

"REMAIN CALM this taxi has altered your destination to get you medical help

Neither confusion nor pain could obscure Micah's problem with medical help. Medical help knew what time it was! Micah had to salvage his alibi currently being thwarted by an idiot computer chip controlled air cab. How would he convince the limited cognition device to resume course? No amount of cursing seemed to help.

Inspiration finally hit. "Medical help needed a 1327 Sagamore Terrace," he said more calmly than he felt

Again Micah was slammed forward and then sideward as the taxi dealt with the new data. His wrist was now sending waves of white-hot pain up his arm. Finally Micah managed to get himself to a sitting position. He searched desperately for some way to outwit the device that still trapped him.

"ASSENDING TO CLEAR MOUNTIANS, AUDITORY DISCOMFORT IS POSSIBLE. WOULD YOU CARE FOR SOME GUM?"

Slowly Micah lifted his mangled finger from the drawer and cradled the selling appendage in his good hand. "No thank you" he managed quietly. The drawer slammed shut.

THE OLD AND THE BEAUTIFUL

Only when Micah tried to move did the last evening's events come flooding into his consciousness; pain brought instant awareness. There was still stiffness in his wrist this morning and a single massive ache throughout his body. The drug had let him strain muscles beyond their current abilities. His broken finger was now splinted and wrapped but most swelling and pain had been removed last evening. Laura was a truly gifted empathic healer well before her artistry had garnered her fame.

Morning sunlight was weaving gold into Laura's usually cinnamon hair. She was twenty-four, talented, strikingly attractive, and, discounting her dedication to him, manifestly intelligent. He knew the infatuation was foolish, even futile. He also knew it was mutual. There was much they could never share across the years between them. She could have her pick of younger suitors offering all that there should be in a loving relationship. Micah knew he should insist she do just that but couldn't bare the absence of the overwhelming comfort and profound inner peace of her company. Both being psychic, Micah hoped she received the same from him. The entire universe could go pound sand but Alero, his friend and her great uncle, would have to be told.

Micah disengaged the covers and found his robe. He stole quietly out the French doors into the formal garden. Laura Pruitt had stamped her home and property with her love of ancient arts. Fruits, vegetables, and textured protein growths populated the beds among the paved pathways fountains and arbors. A profusion of colors and aromatics sated his senses nearly as pleasantly as Laura herself.   He most appreciated that her superbly pleasing creation met nearly every food need of the household as well. After some time of leisurely appreciation, Micah selected two tallow fruit and moved toward the kitchen entry.

To his surprise Laura was there, similarly robed, retrieving cutlery and bowls for the breakfast. How long had he lingered? "Good choice," she remarked, pointing at the fruit with spoons. She arranged each setting at the table.

"Oh Yah," Micah glanced at the tallow depositing one in each bowl and seated himself gingerly, "seemed rite!" He noted, a little shamefully, the puffy discoloration in her right hand from healing him. He would never ask someone else to pay the price for his foolishness; particularly her and yet that is just what had happened. "I wish I hadn't been so stupid about this whole thing," he said

"Stupid?" She asked. "I was rather impressed by your quick thinking in the taxi," she actually giggled while taking her seat. Micah just grunted and shoveled a spoonful of Tallow into his mouth. "As for the rest, well it is kind of romantic being the alibi for my gangster boyfriend."

"Only my stupidity made that necessary," said Micah sincerely irked at himself.

"Master Micah Janis admits a mistake. Let me call the broadcast news." How could she not poke fun at him? She might never again have him in this position. He had shared his astounding conclusion and strenuous adventure to explain the need for an alibi. The Darrel creating Darrel part was still hard to swallow despite sensing the conviction in Micah's mind. The drug assisted escape certainly impressed her but a comedy writer couldn't think up the hilarious trauma in and with the air cab. "Warp master verses Taxi the fight of the century," Laura couldn't resist using her best fake commentator's voice.

Micah snorted around his spoon. His face contorted into an angry scowl only to quickly melt into an amused smile. "Woman it is unfair to read my actual feelings when I'm trying to appear upset. If everyone did that my reputation as a cantankerous genius would be shot."

The vidphone buzzed from the other room. Micah turned as Laura rose. "It's too early for uncle Alero so It's probably time for my act." She said

Micah could hear her calmly activate the connections. "Please forgive the robe but it is quite early for wrong numbers" she said

"Miss Pruitt I'm Damian Tyler of guild security…………"

"The caller ID told me that which is why I'm sure you have the wrong number. I'm neither a warp artist or guild employee Mr. Tyler"

"Yes mam I understand that and I do apologize for the hour but it is rather urgent that we locate Master Micah Janis

"I do know Master Janis but as you can see I'm clearly not him," without preamble she flicked the disconnection put her hands to her mouth like a child with a secret and beamed at Micah who stood smiling and shaking his head in the door way.

"I think you managed to act a lot like me.'" said Micah

"Wasn't I just so full of myself? She asked strolling back toward the table. The videophone buzz stopped her stride.

She turned toward the screen and announced ", It's the guild again" seating herself she made the connection. "Mr. Tyler I…."

"I'm Blythe Hutchinson, Mr. Tyler's boss. Now Miss Pruitt. I truly apologize for our awareness of your ahhh friendship with Master Janis but as it happens we do know. If by any chance he is visiting now it is rather imperative I speak with him."

Micah had been right. They did know. He had mentioned this man by name and he called so quickly that he must have been standing next to the first man. Laura hesitated and then said, "He does happen to be visiting. I'll see if he is available." She paused the connection. The Guild was the only government on Loraine and if they had wanted to they could still ease drop on most videophones. Of course since hers was an antique that was not possible. Micah and she paused, passing each other in the archway between rooms.

"Perfect" he said squeezing her shoulder. "Both more stalling and less evasion would have given away that we expected the call." He kissed her forehead and replaced her at the phone. "Hutchinson I think your just showing off calling me here where no one is supposed to know I hide out" he offered the solemn face on the screen.

"Not my intention sir. We have a serious security breach in which you have been implicated."

"I can't imagine how," Micah feigned innocence.

" I'll do you the honor of being direct," said the image. We have detained a data clerk from the lab section who insists you bribed him to provide unreleased information on our recent transwarp fatality; Not Master Hawshaw but a young crewman."

"I honestly would have no interest in a crewman" said Micah knowing that the statement was perfectly true if technically evasive, "but Master Hawshaw was a boyhood friend and had I thought of it I might have sought more information on his death by calling your boss. It seemed rather straight forward though and no need for subterfuge occurred to me."

The face of Blythe Hutchinson seemed to twitch momentarily on the phone. "Master Janis we have your phone records which show a call from you condo to this clerk last night. Do you still wish to deny involvement?"

Micah sat more erectly in his seat. "I don't wish or need to deny anything but as I made no such call I can't help you. It more seems now that you could help me by finding out who might have been in my condo when I was here. Do you know if they took anything?" he added for effect.

The twitch was back "Exactly when did you arrive at Sagamore Terrace?"

"Approximately fifteen fifteen, when was your phone call?" Micah challenged

"Can you prove that?"

" I don't believe I need to but asking if I could tells me your times don't mesh." Micah knew he needed the correct amount of indignation to sell this. "I would have thought the head of Guild security would have had the forethought to check with the cab data logs before accusing a founder of.... what would that be? Oh yes corrupting a lab tech. Do I need to tell Director Daniels to put a better leash on his head gumshoe?

Blythe's face was flushing red "Well I didn't mean to imply....

Micah broke the connection affecting a growl. He didn't move. He breathed deeply and seemed to slump slack-jawed into the chair. It was time to solve this puzzle.

Laura recognized Micah's condition. She had seen it before without the dread it produced in her now. It wasn't seizure or stroke as an observer might suspect, just that unassailably focused concentration technique called Postulation. In that state setting his robe on fire would produce little response.

She worried that Micah was planning to create a younger version of himself, as had his friend. She feared, more precisely truly expected, a similar fatal outcome. She was uncertain if she could dissuade him but positive that she would make no effort to do so. She would not risk altering the man for her own comfort. In just a few minutes he would emerge from this state determined to either quell or justify her growing dread.

Micah thought about how strange it was that he would even attempt such a thing. He had never minded aging. He treated the years like costumes, affectations on the public role he was always perfecting. Age was part of life and life hadn't mattered for decades. What mattered was the Warp.

In his youth, the Warp's harmonic reality, alone, engenders his ardor. He seeks nothing from it but the stimulating balm of its presence. Micah had found no experience, no drug, no adventure, and few people sufficiently engaging to value being alive. There was the warp, a few worthwhile friends and him. All else was contrived distractions. Now, however, he lived a humiliating denunciation of those years and attitudes. By experiencing the intensely engaging delicious torturer of Laura Pruitt, life had attained consequence. He wanted it and he wanted it in her company.

PICKING UP THE PERPETRATOR

Director Daniels settled in for the flight to Sagamore Terrace. After learning Micah had chartered a transwarp flight for only himself, Blythe had wanted to detain him. Jack knew this was a probable career ending action; he could not hang on any one else. It was a tenuous string of minimal evidence and multiple suppositions, which convinced him Micah was dangerous. What Jack suspected was an absolute danger to the artist, probably the guild, and possibly the actual fabric of space-time itself. Even the most famous, perhaps the most talented living human must be prevented from pulling the plug on everyone else's reality.

The physicists had not agreed but most favored the alternative universe theory. The younger Darrel would have been sucked into this universe by some process ignited in the warp by his older namesake. They even speculated it could be the act of dying in postulation in Warp contact. Why not? Nearly everything about the warp was unfathomable, speculative at best, so anything could be true. Ignorance seemed a convenient hook to hang their theory on.

His thoughts were interrupted by the cabs voice. "Ascending to clear mountains would you like some gum?" A small metallic drawer sprung open"

"No thank you" jack responded and returned to his musings as the drawer retreated. The panel reported having dismissed <u>wormhole matter accretion</u> because a "Newtonian mater-energy debt" was still considered impossible. Besides no impact could be detected in what they could scan of the universe. So they accepted that a younger alternate universe Darrel had slipped into our space-time only to perish needlessly. They suggested that Master Hawshaw death was a poorly timed coincidence or a mental slip provoked by sensing the other self. Either could undeniably produce deadly consequences while facing the warp.

The beauty of their suggestions was that since proof was unattainable it was equally unnecessary. Jack snorted his derision. For them it was Darrell killed Darrell or inversely Darrell killed Darrel. Why shouldn't the conclusion be as crazy as the whole stupid situation?

Jack's gut didn't subscribe to any of it excepting that part about the Warp killing Darrell the elder. In his scenario the suited body was a construct, which failed to ever be alive. Master Hawshaw rendered DR. Frankenstein a bumbling amateur. No hacking and sewing body parts simply will them into being from the Warp.

The scenery below was breathtaking. Most of planet Lorain remained unaltered by the few humans occupying her. Numbers stayed low because the warp was barrier enough to the public who knew of its terrifying dangers. Expansion away from the port city's infrastructure required all buildings to be autonomous in comfort systems and power. No sewer systems, power grid, or roads had ever disturbed the planets face. The Warp Art economy caused non-involved people to migrate toward the Federation's unlimited potential. That Loraine remained a pristine verdant planet was gratifying to Jack.

Ahead, he was surprised to see, an other taxi apparently leading the way toward his destination. It was already much lower and definitely heading for the estate appearing below. All taxis were owned by the guild and Jack could have easily learned if that one had the same destination. No need to bother checking as it was already below cruse height on landing approach. His own cab followed.

Even before his door opened the Guild director could see the lovely Laura Pruitt exiting her formal garden toward the taxi. Sure enough Master Micah Jannis trailed her. Jack positioned himself between the cabs and their approach.

"Director Denials" Laura greeted "I'm afraid we are off to a previous engagement but do let's pick an other time to get together." With that she turned and entered the cab.

Ignoring her Jack raised a hand like an ancient traffic cop stepping in front of the old Warp artist. "Master Jannis I'm afraid I must detain you"

"You'd have to compel me and I don't think you want the hassles that might follow," said Micah

"Both are true and as much as I dislike it both are fact. You are officially compelled as a material witness to defined crimes." Now it was irrevocable. Jack had taken unthinkable step of officially detaining Lorain's most famous resident.

"You're requiring me to accompany you rite now?" questioned Micah.

"Let's get it over with," said Jack. He watched the old man's eyes challenging him. God people could wither under that stare but the stakes were too high for him to cave in now.

"It's your funeral son" said Micah raising a finger for a moments reprieve. "Just go ahead,' he said to Laura." "I'll ether catch up in a wile or let you know why I don't" with that he nodded toward the director and closed her door.

The pair watched Laura take off and entered the remaining taxi. Daniels gave instructions for the stadium towers destination and settled back. In his youth he had imagined sitting next to this preeminent artist as an apprentice. No other master seemed worth his consideration or his gifts. Jack was not humble. Nor was Micah. Each contained an unapologetic self-assurance that permitted neither boasting nor effacement. Jack didn't understand Micah's refusal to take apprentices but he had accepted it.

In the first moments of silence between them Micah was on the same subject. This man had pledged to him on three separate Quarannums despite the master taking the unprecedented step of offering to have whoever else Jack might chose accept his apprenticeship. "Damn you son you've got too much talent to waste," He had said. "I'm not taking apprentices ever so move on" Why had he not?

"Do I have to wait to know what you want?" asked Micah

"If we can dispense with the fencing I'm pretty sure you know what my concerns are." Jack hoped being direct and candid would elicit the same from his hero. It got silence for a few moments. Micah's features went slack and Jack was becoming concerned. The episode was over quickly and Micah turned sharp eyes on the younger man.

"Ok young Mr. Denials" began Micah "I can admit to two petty crimes for which you'll never get support to ground me. Do you think you know them?"

Jack smiled "there's bribing the lab tech, and I'm guessing tampering with an air cab."

Guessing?

"I haven't even checked on that but reviewing you conversation with Blithe I became convinced you must have."

Micah smiled at this reminder of the man's exceptionally nimble mind. Then he experienced instant rage for the very same reason. Long ago Micah had realized the exceptional artist Jack could have been. "You stubborn shit why did you never enter the art?" It was an impulsive change of subject but Micah was genuinely furious at the waste of talent performing only bureaucratic BS.

Jack was taken aback by the intensity of that left-handed compliment. "Because of a stubborn shit of a Master who wouldn't teach me" said Jack. Both men's chests heaved as if recovering from exertion. Jack was surprised at his intense emotions produced that effect. It was also a revelation to Jack that Micah resented his absence from Warp art. Strangely too it offered a perverse comfort as well.

"Yes smart ass" Micah resumed the previous conversation, "Those were the ones. Now are you going to try and hold me on them?"

"Just until the flight you chartered either leaves of stands down." Said jack

"There's no Guild rule against Chartered Warp transit," said Micah indignantly

"There's no rule about destabilizing space-time but I'm reluctant to let you try." Jack retorted

"Ah so you've figured out the whole enchilada. Aren't we the clever one?" Micah jibed. But his sarcasm was quickly replaced by gentle words. "Jack there are all kinds of potential problems with Darrel's plan and I'll admit to possibilities I don't foresee. There is, how ever, zero danger to universal integrity. If you had any time at Warp you would know that. You couldn't explain it but you would know."

Director Daniels studied Micah's face a while chewing over the apparently sincere statement. "Micah it is something I would have to know absolutely before I ever let you into a postulation chamber again. Fair or not, true or not, as you observed; I can't know that." He sighed deeply "So you are grounded"

"Well that's a turd in the punch bowl isn't it?"

They sat silently. Strange how now after years they had truly communicated for the first time. Clearly each had real respect and true anger for the other but they were at loggerheads with no path forward.

The taxi's speaker came to life as they neared the port city. "ASSENDING TO CLEAR MOUNTIANS. AUDITORY DISCOMFORT IS POSSIBLE. WOULD YOU LIKE SOME GUM??"

Micah indicated the drawer in front of the young director with one hand and pointed to his ears with the other. "Would you mind?" he asked

"OH Of course" said jack reaching into the opening.

"No gum!" yelled Micah. Jack started to turn his head with Micah's outburst but jerked it back when the drawer slammed on his finger. He shot off the seat with the pain dazing himself in the collision with the taxi's roof. Micah's rabbit punch at the base of his skull sent all the pain away.

The old artist caught and cradled the unconscious director. "Gum please" he said. Micah gently laid Jack across the seat and gave the spaceport destination change to the cab. He would have to apologize some day.

WARPED MIND

"Laura I don't have time to discuss it. The warp is only minutes away and I've been convincing captain Larry to ignore Guild recall orders."

"No discussion" she said "this is all on you. I just need you to know that I find no defect in us; or more specifically you. Not in your passions, your mind, your arms or your age. So don't use my imagined discontent as motivation for this plan. You already know that I fear this. That is it. That's all I need you to know." She lowered her face and eyes.

Micah placed hands on both her shoulders. She looked up with glistening eyes, imploring something of him but she said nothing. Could he tell her? Did he have time? "You are right about us being superlative beyond improvement except in one regard; Duration! We've never said the word love but there is no other even remotely apt to us. Lovers make lots of gratuitous claims about futures they can't know. By the strength of how important you are to me I will do the same. I will not be separated from you!"

Micah stopped as a sudden knot formed in his throat and tears sprang to his own eyes. Repeated attempts to clear his throat seemed destined to failure so he pushed on through a cracking voice. "As foolish and empty as it may sound I promise you two things. First this is my selfish wish for more of you, more of us. It is not some presumed noble gift to you. Second is that I will not fail. My promise is to be with you until we both look as bad as I do now."

She fell into his arms absolutely gratified. She remained uncertain of Mica's success but was reassured that his feelings mirrored her own, so completely. In this moment that was enough. They Separated, exchanged gazes weighted with emotions beyond words, and finally Micah spun and headed for the postulation chamber. Twice this day Micah had abandoned his cultivated grumpy image for honest emotional communication. Unchecked such things would change his whole persona.

Postulation chambers are Spartan. They are soundproofed, monochromatic presentation, of walls, floors, and ceiling with one cushioned bench the size of a double shower. Their bareness is by design so as not to distract a mind in need of absolute concentration. Micah settled into his preparations. He relaxed into a sense of being over weighted relinquishing control of his voluntary muscles awareness of them could be a distraction. Deep cleansing breaths became shallow and rhythmic also leaving his unconsciousness as he sought his center. The Warp was near.

For Micah organized sequential postulations had always been effortless. He only needed to determine what he wished from the warp and the intricate essential road map to execution of that vision, sprang fully formed into his mind. Other artist agonized over that process, painstakingly detailing and double-checking each critical sequence envying his fortunate mental quirk. Vain in other ways, Micah acknowledged, appreciated, and trusted that ability without pride. Now, however, he challenged himself to examine with unfamiliar persistent effort just how to create the intricacies and harmonies of specialized organs and processes within a living body. He found several effective, and seemingly workable, ways to proceed. He knew Darrel would have found similarly effective means. Why then was he dead? Had he been so intent on form and systems that he neglected to initiate processes like hart beat, peristalses or breathing? The fatal error was unknowable!

Speculation would have to wait. Postulation was eminent as Micah felt the familiar metal caress of the Warp. He was at peace with structured thoughts as his companions. One by one they centered in his mind. The goal, the myriad processes and essential constituents summoned into existence toward that goal. With him in the warp this day was a thing he had never allowed in before. It wasn't an emotion. That was good. Emotions perverted thoughts; kidnapped them and forced the mind to serve their potent illogic. It was more the sterile knowledge of an emotional construct. Ah yes that promise to Laura. It could stay but take no part in the work.

The companion thoughts each did their part. The construct was complete it's environment was safe for life and critical sustaining processes were started. Micah was conscious of sensing nothing of presence from the young body. Humans all had some mental pressure they brought to bear. Not this one. Not yet. That was to be expected because that pressure was still inside this old body. Alero Pruitt would say it had no soul to sense. Being a bishop now he was almost required to think that way. Well Micah intended to transfer, what ever his soul was, to this new younger self.

Transit was all that remained it was the last of the sequences before his miraculous living artwork was complete. But no sequence or mental construct resided in Micah's mind as to how exactly that was to be done. Many questions would have arisen in him had he not mentally quashed them. Artist's could only afford questions away from the warp. Once any question was clearly formed the mind spontaneously began speculating possible answers. It was reflexive and engaged the warp beyond rational control.

Micha had no process or postulation available beyond the force of absolute will. That must be it. The entirety of his mind aided and amplified by the comfort of the warp would will him into the other body and complete the postulation construct.

JUST LIKE THIS; OH YES !

Micah was less in his body. He relinquished it's significance and assumed his being independent of anything temporal. He would enter the new life container constructed from the warp. The process ignored distance and had no actual motion. What ever his core reality was simply evaporated from the body and felt itself amassing elsewhere. Like the warp itself, he seemed now only a connection between two points not truly adjacent to each-other.

Micah was completely freed from flesh. The sequence of thought required to complete the transfer to his waiting body was ready to trigger but his relationship to his own mind now seemed vague. No experience of his long life prepared him for the sensation occurring. It's only reference was the warp itself. It was a broad gentle caressing pressure on the mind. No in and from the mind! No not even that, it was independent of his mind and yet clearly himself. It was power and beauty beyond resisting and he realized his will was being subsumed in seduction to it. Nothing he had intended seemed worthy of the slightest attention. His thoughts held none of the overwhelming magnificence of his truer self, which offered comfort and confidence without cause or definition? It was enticing without demand that dissolved willful intentions.

Micah's magnificence was expanding to the ancient and ever-lasting form. How had he not realized what he was, what he had always been? He was fantastic. He needed no matter to house him and no time to measure him such things were inconsequential fragmentary constructs. There was relief in freedom from them and regret that they had imprisoned his beauty. Being was wondrous.

In this form thought had no purpose. Attention to anything became realization. He needn't observe, speculate and conclude.

He simply focused and knew. Now he focused on himself. How amazingly perfect and wonderful he was. Well except for that slight blemish on his being. It wasn't worth mentioning accept that it existed and he knew it to be a flaw. It did diminish his perfection. He was not intended to accommodate imperfection. Knowledge of its nature or cure was absent within him.

Another approached. How perfect the being was. Words were not needed but concepts did flow. "Micah so wonderful you are here" it offered.

"Darrel, how perfect that you are eternal too"

"We all are friend"

"How were you freed?" asked Micah.

"Like you, it was the Warp. Darrel acknowledged

"There's some other way? Micah asked

"Death frees everyone of course. Can you imagine we used to fear it?"

"We had no way of knowing our true selves then"

"I don't chose to reduce your glory," began Darrel, "but is that a flaw I'm realizing within you?"

"Ah yes! I had been considering it as you approached. I understand it to be unprecedented in ones like us"

"Truly so. I have no knowledge regarding it's cure my friend"

"I have considered empowering it with more of my self just to better know it."

"Being so magnanimous with lessor reality is wonderful and worthy or your nature. Surely empowering it enough to realize your beauty will correct it. I shall withdraw now and await your completeness."

Once alone Micah granted strength to his flaw. Focus now might offer understanding and it might know him. It was a disquieting attachment to materialism. What possible use was that now? How pathetic, tenacious, and needy this flaw was.

Micah exchanged understandings with this flaw. "You can relax now. We are one and you truly have no need for temporal things."

"Let me finish!" The flaw was desperately pleading.

"It is admirable to seek completeness as I am. Relax into me, as I am the overwhelming majority of us. You must recognize that"

"I must become conscious in the construct. Distraction is deadly!"

"Behold our self this is not distraction but perfection almost. Your objective would contain us longer into contingent reality. We are larger than that."

"I have to finish" it nearly whimpered pathetically.

"Are we not spectacular?"

"Yes but" wined the self-flaw

Patiently Micah conversed with the quasi entity. "I have no awareness of purpose in temporal containment but can't you see that you are what is called a mind. The mind is a remarkable and clever imitation of being and is self aware in a limited fashion. You must see now how it diguises or fails to contain our true self. The reality you recognize is a prison for us. I'm reduced to ignorance and limited influence on you as my only form of existence there. You must perceive the completeness and wonder we could be as one?"

"I do, Yes but I can't fully answer you or I'll loose hold of the warp and the sequence I must finish"

Micah understood the problem to be sincere. I shall hold the portal open and return it to you should you still require that of me." Mind considered the portal a bridge between parts of reality having a side effect of manifesting conscious constructs. Micah accepted mind lacked capacity to know it's actual purpose. Still it was the limited capacity of mind that Micah must persuade. So he held to the arch of creation as promised.

Freed of the absolute desperation of holding contact with the warp, the mind of Micah considered its situation. This other self flooded his awareness with peace and joy, beyond wonder and awe. Of course this entire situation was beyond his experience and only his friend Alero Pruitt had ever considered this possibility. "You seem to be my Soul" it began. "I dismissed any thought of your existence in my youth but can't possibly deny you now. As best I can figure, it is you I sense in the warp. You are what I lingered in there to experience and the Art was my excuse. I love a woman with such intensity it overwhelms me. I do believe we can be orders of magnitude more spectacular than that. Still I must take back the warp and complete the postulation"

"Clearly that isn't best. There is no reason for us to ever accept temporal restriction of our being again" said soul

"There is the promise," Mind offered.

"Promise?"

"I did promise"

"A commitment to an other perfection like ourselves?"

"Exactly"

"Oh dear no!" Soul lamented, "You require the unthinkable. We should become less to be complete. I must agree to temporal consequential confinement because you committed us to complete something of no lasting benefit under those conditions. You have constrained us with that promise! What can, possibly, sustain us through that again?"

"Can love help?" Mind asked

BRING OUT YOUR DEAD

Jack cradled his bandaged hand and waited with the medical team for the seals to cycle open. Best guess was that Micah had died in postulation like his fried Darrel. Fortunately there had been no other body floating outside for Blythe to worry about. The news had been radioed ahead and the media was there in force. The medical team rushed in to retrieve the body.

Jack's hart was like led. He could hear one of the Tridee news anchors setting up the hot story. "Micah Janis the maverick genius Master of Warp art, found dead in a postulation chamber by crew. The loss to the guild, Loraine and the galaxy as a whole is incalculable."

True enough thought Jack but at least the Universe was still working. He had managed to warn the crew to hold Laura in the ship upon landing. She could do without the additional ordeal of public scrutiny and titillating speculations. Were her acquaintance known, she would loose all privacy in her grief. Jack intercepted the stretcher as it emerged from the ship. He knew the action was cliché but he unsealed the body bag. He was assured and horrified to see an ancient, frail, inanimate version of the frustrating senior. He sealed it back up and waved them out.

There was no avoiding question from the press but none of the intrigue of the past days need be revealed. Mostly it centered on the fact of a second founder's death within a week. Yes the circumstances were similar. "No we have no idea why he leased a ship alone but he was Micah Janis cantankerous, irascible, and inscrutable to the end. "Now, as you can imagine, there are things I must attend to" Jack abandoned the cordoned of line of journalists and entered the ship.

He found Laura Pruitt in the crew lounge sipping coffee nearly expressionless. A young crewman was leaning back against the counter with a cup in his hand. "Laura I, well I, just don't know what to say" Jack confessed.

She shook her head. "Mr. Denials I completely understand" she glanced at the crewman and back to Jack. "Some things are beyond words," she said.

"Have you told your uncle?"

"I just couldn't begin to explain it all. I asked him to handle that." She indicated the silent young man. "You don't know how completely bewildered I am."

Jack recognized the crewman's face but couldn't pull up a name or even how or why he knew him. Blithe leaned in with a crew manifest. Jack took it and sat dawn across from Laura. No profound, important, or comforting words occurred to Jack, for such an occasion.

"Do your people need me for anything?" She asked.

"No, not at all, we are good" he assured her. It was both strange and natural that she gently touched his hand. What could one say? As she left, the guild director rose out of respect. He too had no further business here.

"Director Daniels" the crewman spoke

"Yes?' said jack turning to the young man.

"I'd like to share something with you but I need to know that you'll keep it just between us" the man's hand made a circle of the room.

"Well, since I don't really know you, it depends on what it is.

"I'm Em jay and what I want to share is more apology than fact. Perhaps you can promise out of respect to Master Janice," he offered

Reflexively Jack checked the crew manifest. He found an entry penciled onto the bottom, M. J. Goodbody cook, it read. Had Micah decided he was hungry from the exertion of his escape? Jack frowned and looked up. The crewman seemed to be smirking at jack's confusion. Oh well, what could it hurt to humor him? "Alright then, If it's that important to you I can keep an apology secret," he replied.

"Oh thanks Jack. I just need to get this off my chest"

"Yes?" jack prompted, irritated by the man's presumed familiarity.

"I'm really sorry about the finger!"

THE END